#2 Fly Frenzy

Books in the S.W.I.T.C.H. series

#1 Spider Stampede

#2 Fly Frenzy

#3 Grasshopper Glitch

#4 Ant Attack

#5 Crane Fly Crash

#6 Beetle Blast

#2 Fly Frenzy

Ali Sparkes

illustrated by

Ross Collins

MINNEAPOLIS

"SWITCH: Fly Frenzy" was originally published in English in 2011. This edition is published by an arrangement with Oxford University Press.

Darby Creek
A division of Lerner Publishing Group, Inc.
241 First Avenue North
Minneapolis, MN 55401 U.S.A.

Website address: www.lernerbooks.com

Main body text set in ITC Goudy Sans Std. 14/19.
Typeface provided by Monotype Typography.

Library of Congress Cataloging-in-Publication Data

Sparkes, Ali.
Fly frenzy / by Ali Sparkes ; illustrated by Ross Collins.
p. cm. — (S.W.I.T.C.H. ; #02)
Summary: Mad scientist Petty Potts asks her neighbors, twins Josh and Danny, to help with her experiments and when her SWITCH spray turns them into flies, they are able to investigate the sabotage of their mother's garden.
ISBN 978-0-7613-9200-2 (lib. bdg. : alk. paper)
[1. Flies—Fiction. 2. Brothers—Fiction. 3. Twins—Fiction. 4. Science fiction.] I. Collins, Ross, ill. II. Title.
PZ7.S73712Fly 2013
[Fic]—dc23 2012026632

Manufactured in the United States of America
1 – SB – 12/31/12

For Gregory

Danny and Josh (and Piddle)

They may be twins, but they're NOT the same! Josh loves insects, spiders, beetles, and bugs. Danny can't stand them. Anything little with multiple legs freaks him out. So sharing a bedroom with Josh can be . . . erm . . . interesting. Mind you, they both love putting earwigs in big sister Jenny's underwear drawer . . .

Danny

- FULL NAME: Danny Phillips
- AGE: eight years
- HEIGHT: taller than Josh
- FAVORITE THING: skateboarding
- WORST THING: creepy-crawlies and cleaning
- AMBITION: to be a stuntman

Josh

- FULL NAME: Josh Phillips
- AGE: eight years
- HEIGHT: taller than Danny
- FAVORITE THING: collecting insects
- WORST THING: skateboarding
- AMBITION: to be an entomologist

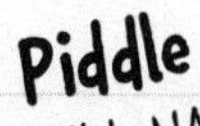

Piddle

- FULL NAME: Piddle the dog Phillips
- AGE: two dog years (fourteen in human years)
- HEIGHT: not very
- FAVORITE THING: chasing sticks
- WORST THING: cats
- AMBITION: to bite a squirrel

Contents

Horror at the Hedge

"Buzz off, you revolting little pest!" Jenny thwacked Danny on the head with her rolled-up magazine.

Josh tried not to giggle. His sister had been reading peacefully for five minutes. She was unaware that Danny was crouched on the back of the sofa behind her. He was rubbing the backs of his hands together, sticking out his tongue, and rolling his eyes madly. A half-eaten cookie in her hand, Jenny hadn't even noticed Josh standing in the doorway. He was taking pictures with his little digital camera.

It was only when Danny started buzzing that things turned ugly.

"Go and play outside, you creepy little horrors!" yelled Jenny. She was fourteen, so she thought she could boss them around. She whacked Danny again. He fell off the sofa and rolled across the living room floor, laughing and buzzing.

Josh tucked his camera into his pocket. He strolled out toward the front yard with his twin brother. "Of course, if you *really* wanted to be a fly, you should have spit stomach acid on her cookie. Then walked all over it until it was mush. *Then* eaten it."

Danny biffed the back of Josh's neat, blond head as they went down the hallway. "And Mom says *I'm* the disgusting one!"

"It's just nature," shrugged Josh. He biffed Danny back on his spiky, blond head. "Flies are amazing. I can show you one under my microscope if you like."

"Yuck! I *don't* like!" shuddered Danny. It was one thing pretending to be an insect to annoy Jenny. He hated the real thing.

"You ate one quite happily a couple of weeks ago," Josh reminded him.

Danny stopped dead on the front doorstep. "I thought we agreed never to talk about that again!"

"Well, yeah, but—"

"NEVER!" said Danny.

Outside, Mom was by the front hedge. She was talking to Mrs. Sharpe from down the street. Mom's garden looked fantastic. It was carefully trimmed and mowed. It was full of flowers, bushes, and little trees, all overflowing with colorful blossoms. The hedge, though, was her real pride and joy. For years she had trimmed and trained it into three little bird shapes along the top. It was a special skill called "topiary," she had explained to Josh and Danny. She called them her "hedge birds."

"Come to help with the weeding, boys?" she asked when she saw them. Mom was in the best garden competition in their town. Last year she'd come in third. This year she was determined to win. Piddle, their terrier dog, had been banned from going anywhere near the front garden. He was shut in the backyard today, out of harm's way.

"Can't see any weeds!" said Josh.

"There are some there," said Mrs. Sharpe. She pointed at the rose bed. "And over by the marigolds. Quite a few really. Of course, my garden is completely weed free now. With only one day to go before judging, I couldn't possibly allow anything wild to start messing it up." She smiled smugly at them all. "Have to make sure I keep the cup again this year, don't I, Tarquin?"

A thin, pale boy of about Josh and Danny's age slithered around from behind his mother. He gave their garden a look of great disdain. "I think your trophy is quite safe, Mother," he said, in a high-pitched voice.

"Well," said Mom. She twisted a dead rose bloom off its stalk with some force. "How nice to

have a supportive son, Mrs. Sharpe."

"He *is* a darling," sighed Mrs. Sharpe. "And did I tell you that he scored top in his whole school for math this week? He's Mommy's little genius!" She patted Tarquin's neatly parted hair. "Of course, not every child can be a genius, can they?" She smiled pityingly at Josh and Danny. "But that doesn't matter, *does it*?"

Danny made being sick noises. Tarquin made ugly faces at them.

"Well, must keep working!" Mom knelt down and drove her trowel viciously into the soil. "We never know *who* might win this year, do we?"

"Don't we?" smirked Mrs. Sharpe. "Well, have fun trying. It really is quite a *nice* little garden . . . " And she stalked off with her son. He was still sticking his tongue out at Josh and Danny.

"Come on, you two," said Mom. "Pay no attention to the genius! Weeding, please!"

Josh and Danny worked their way along the wall. They pulled out very tiny weeds and threw them into Mom's wheelbarrow. "Wee-aargh!" shrieked Danny, wildly flapping his hand. A small spider dropped off it and scuttled away.

"You know, I'm surprised you haven't got over your fear of spiders," said Josh, quietly. "Considering you've *been* a spider."

"*DON'T* remind me!" Danny looked around warily for more eight-legged foes. "I'm trying to forget it ever happened."

"What—that we got hit by Miss Potts's S.W.I.T.C.H. spray? And we got changed into spiders, fell down the drain, got rescued by rats. Then we were almost eaten by a toad and a blackbird, and then got made human again—all before dinner?" Josh grinned as Danny narrowed his eyes at him.

"I don't know *how* you can be so calm about it!" grunted Danny, brutally pulling up a dandelion.

"I'm not!" said Josh. "It gives me the shivers just to think about Petty Potts. She's hidden away in her secret lab behind the shed, turning all kinds of poor creatures into bugs just for fun. But it *was* kind of exciting too—wasn't it? And she *did* turn us back again."

"Exciting? It was *terrifying*! I was a *spider*! A spider! I was scared of my *own legs*!"

Josh chucked another handful of weeds into the wheelbarrow. "Well, don't worry. It's all in the past now. We haven't even seen Petty Potts since. And we're never going next door again!"

"Ah!" said Mom to someone at the gate. "Good timing! I'm just about to go to the garden center now. Is it still OK for the boys to come over to your house?"

Danny and Josh looked up from their weeding. Their mouths fell open in horror.

Standing by the hedge was their next-door neighbor: Petty Potts.

Call Me Petty

"NOOOOOO!" shouted Josh and Danny. They stared aghast at the secret scientist who had transformed them into spiders.

"Josh! Danny!" Their mother looked at them crossly. "How can you be so rude?"

"We—we—we mean . . . " gabbled Josh. "We mean we wanted to come along to the garden center with you. Th-that's all . . . "

Danny just gibbered.

"Well, you can't come! I have a lot to do if I'm going to win the contest. I don't need you two running around and climbing up the trellises!" Mom put her hands on her hips. They knew it was no good arguing when she did that. But Danny tried anyway.

"We could help . . . " he began.

"No! You couldn't! I would leave you here, but Jenny's going out. Miss Potts has very kindly offered to babysit you. Now, isn't that nice of her?"

Petty Potts smiled sweetly at them. To Danny she looked like a wolf in a tweed hat and glasses. "Come on in," she said, heading back to her house. "I have cake . . . "

"Right," said their mom. "Off you go then."

"But she's . . . weird!" hissed Danny.

"Nonsense," said their mother. "She's very nice once you get to know her. I know she was always complaining about your noisy playing before. But just recently I think she's become rather fond of you both."

"It's only because she wants to use us for experiments," muttered Danny.

Mom laughed. "You and your crazy ideas, Danny! Now, on your best behavior, please, both of you. What are you waiting for? She said there's cake!"

"DON'T YOU TRY ANYTHING, MISS POTTS!" warned Josh, the moment Petty Potts's front door closed behind them. Her hallway was dark and old-fashioned. It smelled like damp wood.

POTTS

"Oh, do call me Petty. And stop being such a ninny," she said. "I have no intention of wasting good S.W.I.T.C.H. spray on you again. I've already tried it on you and it worked. No need to repeat the experiment."

"Why are you being all nice to Mom, then?" asked Danny, with a suspicious glare.

"I'm just trying to be a good neighbor." She beckoned them down the hall and into her warm kitchen. There was, indeed, an iced sponge cake on the table. And cups of orange pop next to it. Petty sat down at the table. She waved her guests toward two neighboring chairs. "But—all right—if you must know. I *have* been wondering

whether your little spider adventure has had any aftereffects. How have you been?"

"Fine," grunted Danny. He sat down as Josh took the seat beside him. He eyed the cake, tormented. It looked so good but . . . "Have you put something in that?" he asked. "Are you trying to turn us into spiders again?"

Petty stood up and looked at them squarely. "Now, listen. I know you both think I'm some kind of old witch. But I am merely trying to work on my experiments. I didn't ask you to come running into my lab and stand in front of the S.W.I.T.C.H. spray jet, did I?"

"No," said Josh. "But you *were* trying to spray Piddle!"

"I beg your pardon?" Petty raised an eyebrow behind her spectacles.

"Our dog! Piddle! You were trying to spray *him*, weren't you?"

"All right, I'll admit it," she said. She sat back down at the table and cut the cake. "But let's not bicker about it. It would only have been temporary. I promise I won't try to spray Piddle again. Or either of you." She took a big wedge of cake and bit into it. "Sheee?" she said. "It'sh quite shafe to eat!"

The cake was too good to resist. After a few bites, they started to relax. Petty also sipped from one of their cups of pop to prove these weren't full of S.W.I.T.C.H. juice.

"All quite safe. However," sighed Petty. She had a wistful look on her face. "A little part of me was *hoping* . . ."

"Hoping *what*? " asked Josh, his cake frozen halfway to his mouth.

"No—no, it doesn't matter," said Petty. She picked up crumbs by squashing them together on her finger. "Nothing."

" *What*?" demanded Danny.

Petty licked the crumbs off her finger. She eyed them both as if she was adding something up. "Well, the fact is, I need help."

"You're not kidding," grunted Danny.

"I *meant* I need help with my amazing research," said Petty. "I've been working alone for far too long. If I had some assistance . . . Well, put it this way, we wouldn't just be talking about spiders or ants or flies." She paused dramatically. "We'd also be talking about . . . dragons."

Josh and Danny stared at her.

"Close your mouth, Danny," said Petty. "I can see your munched-up cake."

"Dragons?" echoed Josh. "You mean you could make us turn into dragons?"

"Doesn't matter, though, does it?" said Petty, briskly cutting another slice of cake. "Because you don't want anything to do with the S.W.I.T.C.H. Project. It's far too dangerous."

"H-how? How can you turn us into dragons?" gulped Danny.

"Well, in fact, I can't," said Petty. "Not yet. Not until I've found something which I lost. Once I've found it, there will be no stopping me! I will work my way up from insects to reptiles. Maybe even mammals and birds. But not until I have found it."

"Found what?" asked Josh.

Petty peered at them hard. "My memory," she said. Josh and Danny peered back at their weird neighbor, astonished.

"Well, in fact I didn't *lose* it," she went on. "It was destroyed. By Victor Crouch."

"Victor Crouch? Who's he?" asked Danny. This was starting to feel like a very odd guessing game. Petty suddenly drove the cake knife into the table with a vicious crack.

"Victor Crouch and I used to be good friends. We both worked for the government. In the best laboratories in the world, hidden underground somewhere in Berkshire. That's where I first

stumbled upon the formula to create the S.W.I.T.C.H. spray. But I kept the secret to myself. Then Victor discovered my diary, read it, and decided to steal my work!"

She pulled the cake knife out of the table. Danny and Josh flinched as she stabbed it back in again, with even more force. "So he stole my notes, claimed the S.W.I.T.C.H. Project was all his own work. And then . . . he burnt my memory out and got me fired!"

Josh and Danny gulped. "How did he burn your memory out?" breathed Danny.

"Oh—there are all kinds of clever ways to do that!" muttered Petty. "I only know it happened because of my nose."

"Your nose?" queried Josh.

"Yes—it doesn't work properly anymore! And one thing I *do* remember about my old government agency days is that when you burn out part of someone's memory, you mess up their sense of smell too. I can't smell things correctly. This cake smells like cheese. Cheese smells like coal. And so on . . ."

"So how come you're still working on your project then?" asked Josh.

"Well," grinned Petty, "what Victor didn't know was that I had *expected* something like this to happen one day! So I transformed all my notes into a secret code. And then I left fake notes in their place! Just in case someone ever tried to do the dirty on me! The *real* secret code for each S.W.I.T.C.H. Spray is chopped into six parts. And each part is hidden inside one of these." She pulled something from a red velvet box on the table. She held it up to the light. A small cube of glass twinkled in her fingers. Inside it was a hologram of a spider—and some strange symbols in a line beneath it. "It's a S.W.I.T.C.H. formula cube," she said.

"Inside this one is part of the code for what I call the BUGSWITCH Spray. I have the other five of these. The complete set of BUGSWITCH cubes."

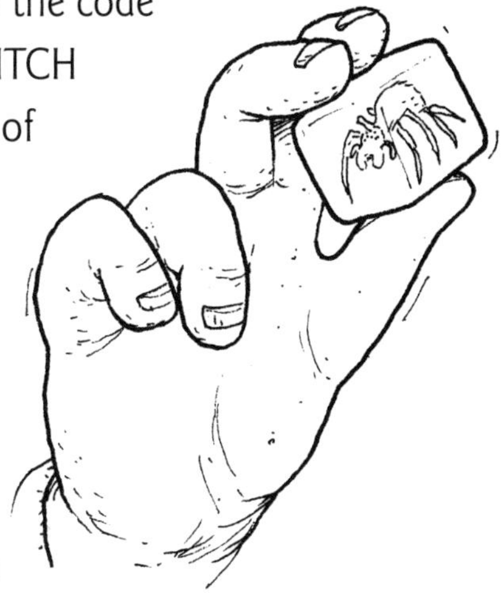

She turned the red velvet box around. They saw five more cubes. They glinted in the light through the kitchen window, each with slightly different holograms.

"That's why I can make BUGSWITCH Spray." She pressed the cube into the dent in the box beside the others and snapped the lid shut. "BUT—there are more! I know there are REPTOSWITCH cubes too! Because I have just one cube in this box. And five empty spaces." She flipped open the green velvet box and held up another cube. This one had a tiny lizard hologram inside it and more strange symbols.

"And there might be mammal cubes! There may even be bird cubes! I can't be sure. I don't know how far I got before Victor Crouch did a smash and grab on my brain. But first of all, I *have* to find the REPTOSWITCH formula hidden in the missing cubes."

She rolled the rather beautiful, single REPTOSWITCH cube around in her palm. She held it closer to Danny and Josh. "So . . . if you *were* to become my assistants and if we were to find all the REPTOSWITCH cubes, . . . who's to say you couldn't find out what it's like to be a *dragon*?"

Bush Ambush

Josh and Danny were silent. They gazed at the glass cube with its holographic lizard. "But," said Josh, after a while, "there's no such thing as a dragon. We know you can do spiders. But they're real. Dragons are just make-believe." Josh knew a lot about wildlife. For an eight-year-old he was really quite an expert. He was quite certain dragons did not exist.

"Well, what about the Komodo dragon?" said Petty.

"OK—there is a Komodo dragon," admitted Josh.

"And a water dragon," added Petty.

"Well, yes—all right! But they're just types of lizards," said Josh. "They can't fly or breathe fire."

"But don't you see, Josh?" said Petty. "I can make humans turn into spiders! Why not go a step further? Mix up a bird formula with the reptile formula? Maybe I could create a DRAGOSWITCH Spray too? Wouldn't you like to find out?"

Josh and Danny started to bite their lips and tap their fingers against the tabletop. It was an amazing idea.

"Oh come on!" urged Petty, putting the cube back into its box. "You can't tell me you don't want to try out being a dragon one day! And all you have to do is help me find the missing cubes! They can't be far away. I wouldn't have hidden them in Timbuktu! They're bound to be close to my lab. So you could help me look! And maybe try out a few sprays with me. I promise you'll be quite safe!"

It was the look on Petty's face that made Josh and Danny stop the finger tapping and lip biting. She looked like a spider herself now, beckoning them into her web.

"No," said Josh.

"No," agreed Danny. "You're nuts!"

Petty opened her mouth.

And then there was a loud, anguished scream. It came from outside. Danny, Josh, and Petty

Potts ran down the hallway. They were out at the front of the house in seconds. Mom was outside, staring at her hedge.

The lovingly tended hedge birds had been cut off.

"Who would have done such a thing?" gasped Mom. She gazed woefully at the mangled stumps of twig that were left. There was no sign of the hedge birds, other than a scattering of their leaves on the pavement.

"Well, you don't have to be a genius to work that out," said Petty Potts. "Even though I am one. It'll be Mrs. Sharpe. Or her loathsome son."

"No!" Mom looked shocked.

"Well, you don't think she keeps winning Best Garden every year by playing fair, do you?" asked Petty. "Her garden's not that good."

"But—but how could we ever prove it?" gasped Mom.

"Well, unless you happened to have a video camera aimed at your garden for the last hour, you can't!" said Petty. She looked at Josh and Danny with a wide, innocent smile. "If only you could somehow get into their house and be a fly on the wall . . ."

Josh and Danny stared back at her. She wasn't really suggesting . . . ? She didn't really mean . . . ? Did she?

"Shall we go back inside, while your Mom phones the police?" asked Petty.

"Thanks, Miss Potts," sighed Mom. "But I don't think the police can help now. The judging is tomorrow. It's not even as if I can cheat and wire the birds back on. They're gone! But if you could have Josh and Danny a little longer, I think I need to sit down and have a quiet cup of tea."

"You didn't really mean that—did you?" demanded Danny as soon as they shut Petty's front door. "About being a fly on the wall?"

"Now remember," said Petty, leading them through the kitchen and out into the back garden. "I told you that I would never spray you with BUGSWITCH again. Funnily enough, I do happen to have the bluebottle housefly variety all set up to go, right now. But I would never spray it on you."

Josh and Danny followed her through waist-high weeds, across her garden, and into the shed. "Or ever make you press the time-delay button that enables you to start the spray. Then you could get yourself inside the special spray tent before it goes off."

"Don't listen to her! Don't go into her shed!" said Danny. Josh got a glittery look in his eyes.

Petty stepped into the shed. She walked past the rarely used lawnmower, the spade, and the rake. She pushed aside the old sacking on the back wall to reveal a red metal door. She turned the handle.

It opened on to a short flight of dark steps, leading down to a gloomy corridor. Danny couldn't stop Josh from following her through.

"But we could get over into Mrs. Sharpe's house, though—really easily!" said Josh. They went down

the corridor. It smelled like old bricks and earth and other more peculiar scents from a room at the end. "Her garden backs onto ours. We could fly in through her window, have a look around for evidence, and then get back again in two minutes!"

"But . . . it's so dangerous!" gasped Danny.

"Well, you don't have to come," said Josh. "But nobody messes with my mom's hedge and gets away with it! Not if I can help it!"

"Of course, I could never recommend that you come in here," went on Petty. They arrived in her lab. It was full of odd machinery, gadgets, and a square tent of plastic sheeting right in the middle. "Or come into the control booth and hit any of the buttons. That would be the very last thing you would want to do."

Josh went into the booth after her. It was the size of a large cupboard. It was lit with the green glow of three computer screens, covered in numbers. In front of the screens was a large control panel. The buttons on it were marked with various creepy-crawly shapes, like those in the BUGSWITCH cubes. He saw the spider button next to a beetle button, just down from an ant button. Below that was a button with a bluebottle shape on it. A fly. A fly on the wall . . .

Josh didn't waste any time. He hit the button.

There was a sudden humming noise. A blue light came on in the plastic tent. He ran across and pushed his way inside it through a narrow gap. The hissing started, and a fine yellow mist sprayed across his legs.

"Josh! What are you doing?" yelled Danny.

"It's OK—it won't take long. Back in two minutes," said Josh.

Danny slapped his forehead and groaned. He knew he couldn't let Josh go on his own. "This is such a bad idea!" he muttered. He stepped into the tent with his brother.

"Oh my. What have you done?" said Petty, cheerfully. "Now, remember, it's only temporary. You'll need to get back fast. You don't want to revert to boys while you're still in Mrs. Sharpe's house."

Josh began to feel peculiar. The plastic sheets around him swished into a whirly pattern. Then they shot upward, as if he was falling. Yet he could still feel the concrete floor under his two feet. Ah—no. Scratch that. Under his six feet.

Bathroom Soup

"WAHAAY!" shouted Josh. Danny towered above him like a giant. His nearby foot, in its muddy sneaker, was the size of a truck. Josh seemed to be looking through thousands of little hexagonal lenses. And he could see all around him without even moving. He was bug-eyed!

"WHEEE-RRRE IIIIIzzzzz HEEEE?" he heard Danny bellow in a deep loud voice. It vibrated right through his highly tuned black body.

Josh felt his six feet move off the floor. He realized that the ticklish feeling on his back was coming from the whirring of his own two wings.

"WEEE-HEEE!" he gurgled, full of excitement. He rose up in the air like a Harrier Jump Jet. A moment later, he was staring, amazed, into Danny's huge face. His own blue-black body

was reflected in the two gigantic shiny orbs of his brother's eyes. His new bluebottle head was almost triangular in shape. His immense bulging golden eyes softened the corners. Two tiny stubby feelers (called palps, he knew, from his wildlife books) wiggled where his nose used to be, with a little spiky antenna on each. Josh stuck out his tongue. What emerged from his chin area was a black sticklike thing that bent in the middle like an elbow. A spongy blob was on the end.

"Woo-hoo!" shouted Josh. "I've got a proboscis!"

"JOOOSH?" boomed Danny's humongous face, the fly's eyes crinkling up in wonder. And then Danny disappeared into a tiny dot, way down on the floor. A few seconds later, he was up in the air next to Josh.

"Josh! Josh!" he squeaked. His bug eyes bulged with amazement. "I can fly!"

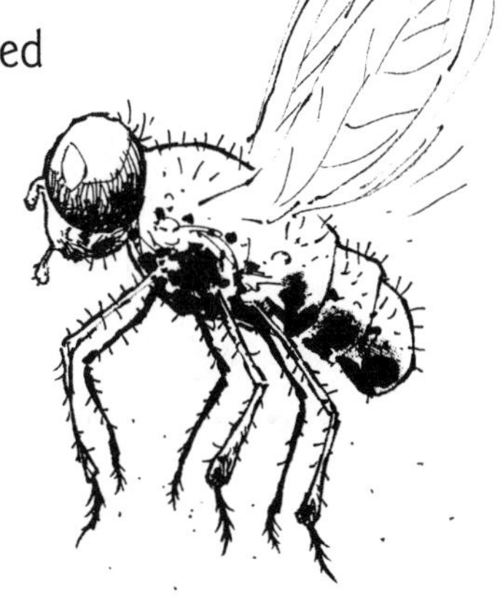

"It's a buzz, isn't it?" giggled Josh. He flicked his peculiar mouthparts about with excitement.

"And I can see my own butt!" marveled Danny. "Without turning my head around!"

"Well, that makes it all worthwhile!" chortled Josh.

"It's your special fly eyes! They're designed so you can see all the way around, in case of predators. Now! We have to hurry. Follow me. I know the way to Mrs. Sharpe's house."

He could just make out Petty slowly waving a huge pink hand at them. He shot out through the gap in the plastic tent. He flew past the open lab door, back up the steps to the shed, and out into Petty's garden. Danny was just behind him. It didn't look so much like a garden now. More like an immense jungle with a tangled mass of exotic trees spreading below them as far as their bug eyes could see. The jungle sent up intense smells of greenery, flower pollen, and something gorgeously brown and sticky from the other side of the fence. It was near Piddle's basket.

Danny whirled about in astonishment. The sky was filled with aircraft, thundering, thudding, zooming, and whining past. "It's an air show!" he yelped. He dodged what looked like a small black and yellow helicopter with a terrifying face. Two blue jets darted past so fast he got spun around in midair.

"Where did all these aircraft come from?"

"They're not aircraft, you dingbat!" said Josh. He hovered up alongside Danny, his dangly black forelegs blowing in the breeze. "They're other insects. Look out for the black and yellow ones. They're wasps. They'd happily eat us if they could. The dragonflies—those blue jets—can be pretty fierce too. But I think they're just looking for girlfriends."

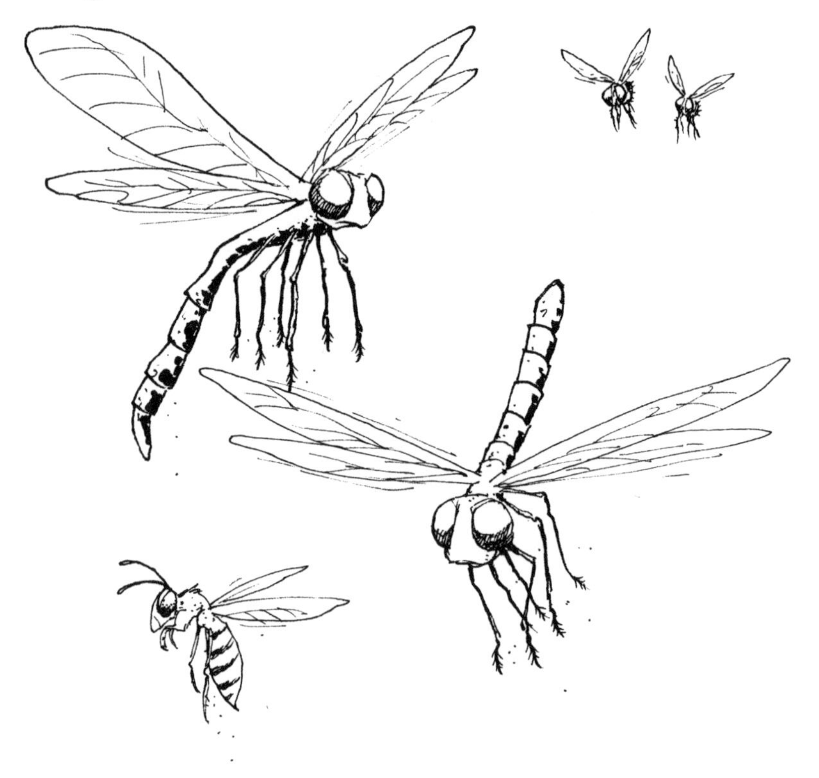

Josh pivoted in the air like an expert pilot. He zoomed off toward some giant trees at the end of the garden. Danny followed. Being a fly felt amazing!

"I can't believe I ever thought flies were annoying!" he called to Josh. He zoomed up behind him and looped the loop. "They're brilliant!" He felt rather guilty about the brilliant flying machine he had pulped against the bedroom wall with a rolled-up comic just last week. And even guiltier about the one he ate when he was a spider.

In no time at all, they were across the back fence, between the huge tree trunks, and over Mrs. Sharpe's neat and pretty back garden. They headed for the house. Now they had to get inside and find out whether the Sharpes had ruined their mom's hedge.

They shot in through an open upstairs window. They found themselves in a vast bathroom. Huge vats of smelly potions sat on a glass shelf. It made Josh's sensitive antennae twitch. A boulder-sized lump of greeny-white stuff on the basin sent up an intense minty whiff. Toothpaste! Josh realized.

"Everything smells ten times stronger, doesn't it?" he shouted to Danny. "Danny? Oh—yuck! Danny! Stop that!" shouted Josh.

Danny jumped and rose up with a shudder.

"You weren't really going to drink that, were you?" asked Josh.

"No—of course not!" spluttered Danny. "I—I didn't realize I was on the edge of the toilet, did I? I didn't know what it was . . . It just smelled . . . "

"Kind of . . . tasty?" muttered Josh. "Like bathroom soup."

Danny pivoted around in the air to stare at his brother. "It's because we're flies, isn't it?"

"Yep," said Josh. "To a fly, pee is soup."

"And that really nice smell from near Piddle's basket . . . ?"

"Let's just get going, shall we?" said Josh, briskly. "We've got work to do!"

They flew around the edge of the bathroom door. They dropped through the warm updraft of air from downstairs. Now they could hear voices. Heavy, slow, and human.

Following the voices, which vibrated around them, they arrived in the kitchen. It smelled incredibly sweet. Mrs. Sharpe was making cakes. Tarquin was with her. He was sitting at the kitchen table.

"Shhh!" said Josh. "Let's wait here and listen for a while. See if they own up to chopping up Mom's hedge."

And then the room flipped over.

Snot Funny

It didn't seem strange that the room had flipped over. To Josh and Danny, now standing on the ceiling, being upside down felt like the most natural thing in the world.

"This is so cool!" said Danny. "And ooooh, that cake mix smells so good!"

"Sshh! We need to listen to them!" said Josh. It wasn't easy. Just like the last time, when they'd shrunk into spiders, human speech sounded much deeper and slower than usual. After a while, though, Josh felt his quick fly brain adapt. He began to understand what Mrs. Sharpe and Tarquin were saying.

"Good work, Tarquin," said Mrs. Sharpe. "Are you sure nobody saw you?"

"Of course not, Mother!" sniffed Tarquin. "I am not an idiot, you know!"

"Good. Just as long as you're sure. Even though my garden is obviously the best in town, the judge could have been charmed by those dreadful tacky topiary birds. Now there's not much chance of that! Did you hide them, like I said? I wouldn't put it past her to cheat and wire them back on."

"Yes, Mother. They're in the front room."

Josh and Danny gasped. Petty was right!

"The front room? Are you crazy? What if the judge comes early and finds the evidence all over the carpet?" Mrs. Sharpe waved her wooden spoon around in fury. A large blob of cake mix splodged onto the floor. A wonderful scent hit Danny like a wave. He just couldn't help himself. He dropped down from the ceiling, turning a somersault in the air. He buzzed straight for the floor.

"Danny!" called Josh. "We haven't got time for snacks! We have to find Mom's hedge birds!"

"I can't . . . help . . . myself . . ." wailed back Danny. He landed on the pale yellow blob, which rose up like a small hill from the red floor tile. His proboscis stuck out of his face and squelched down into the glorious squidgy mess.

Something gooey shot out of the end of his proboscis, making the cake mix go squishier still. Now he could suck it up like a milk shake. Oooh! It was delicious!

Josh landed beside Danny with a plop. "Come on," he said. "Time to go!" But before he could say another word, his own proboscis had shot out and was busy spitting goo out too. A second later, Josh was also sucking up cake mix and fly-spit smoothie.

Then there was a sudden whoosh of wind behind them. A terrifying thrumming noise. Josh and Danny looked up to see a huge orange crisscross square hurtling toward them.

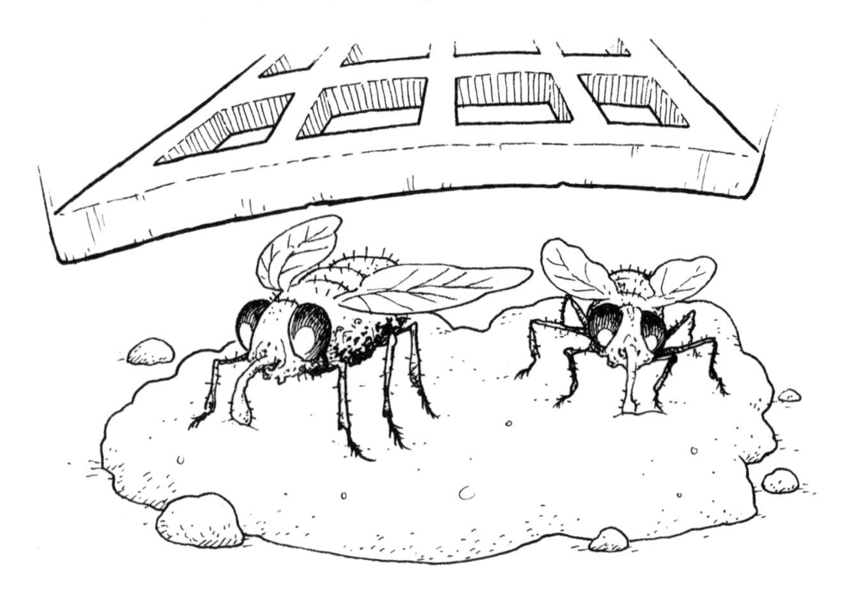

"ARRRGH!" yelled Danny, shooting high into the air. His proboscis snapped back into his face like a pinged rubber band. "It's a flyswatter! They're swatting us!" Josh had figured this out too. He zoomed across the kitchen so fast his vision blurred. Danny flew close behind him, yelling, "GO! GO! GO! GO!"

A second later, they were in the hallway. Then Josh turned left. He flew into the front room. "Look!" he yelled, angrily, pointing with one of his front legs. There on the vast field of swirly red carpet lay three leafy, twiggy birds, cut from Mom's hedge.

Now Tarquin was marching into the room with Mrs. Sharpe at his heels. She still held the flyswatter. Tarquin had a trash bag in his hand.

"Pick them up then," said Mrs. Sharpe. "No—wait. We'll have to pull them to pieces first. Just in case the garbagemen spot them."

And she went to pick up Mom's favorite hedge bird creation.

"NOOOOOOOOOOOO!" yelled Josh and dive-bombed Mrs. Sharpe's face. He aimed for her nose—a huge pink outcrop on the massive pink slab of her face. Before he could rethink the idea, he had shot right up her left nostril.

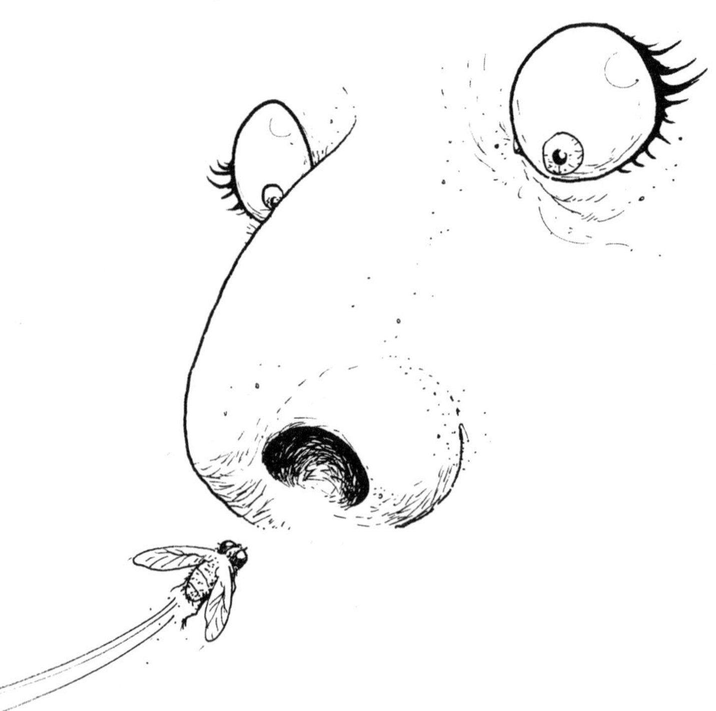

It certainly distracted her. As Josh rolled over in the nasty, windy, hairy cavern, Mrs. Sharpe shrieked and spluttered and sneezed. Josh hurtled back out again in a blast of nose goo.

He ended up stuck to the leather sofa in a green globule. Danny, meanwhile, flew down and shot under the sofa. He zoomed low over the thick clumps of dust and hair and the twisted sculptures of candy wrappers on the shadowy carpet. He aimed for the line of light at the far side. He planned to shoot quickly up the back of the sofa and get ahold of Josh from behind. He didn't want to attract the flyswatter that Tarquin was now twitching about in the air. But just a few inches up the back of the sofa, something pushed hard against Danny's head. It stopped him in flight.

It felt as if he'd flown into the goal during a soccer game. Like a big net. A big, sticky, net. A big, sticky, shivering net. Danny shouted and tried to get back down off the net, but it stuck to him like . . . like . . . like . . . A WEB!

In the dusty darkness, eight red eyes suddenly lit up. Eight long, hairy legs began to pick their way down the silken ropes toward Danny.

Danny didn't know as much about wildlife as Josh did. But he knew this much—the spider was coming to meet him for lunch.

And Danny was on the menu!

A Narrow Squeak

Josh had just managed to slither out of the giant booger. He was edging away over the back of the sofa when he heard Danny scream. He could only just hear it over Mrs. Sharpe. She was still sneezing and gasping and blowing her nose noisily. Josh peered down from the top of the sofa and saw a terrifying sight.

A huge hairy spider was flipping Danny over and over with its legs and wrapping him up in silk. Danny was struggling hard. But he was no match for the spider. A female, judging by her size and skinny palps, thought Josh.

"Look!" he shouted down. "This is all a mistake! He's not actually a fly at all, and neither am I!" The spider paused, looked up at Josh, and narrowed all eight eyes. Then she came running for him, obviously wanting him for dessert.

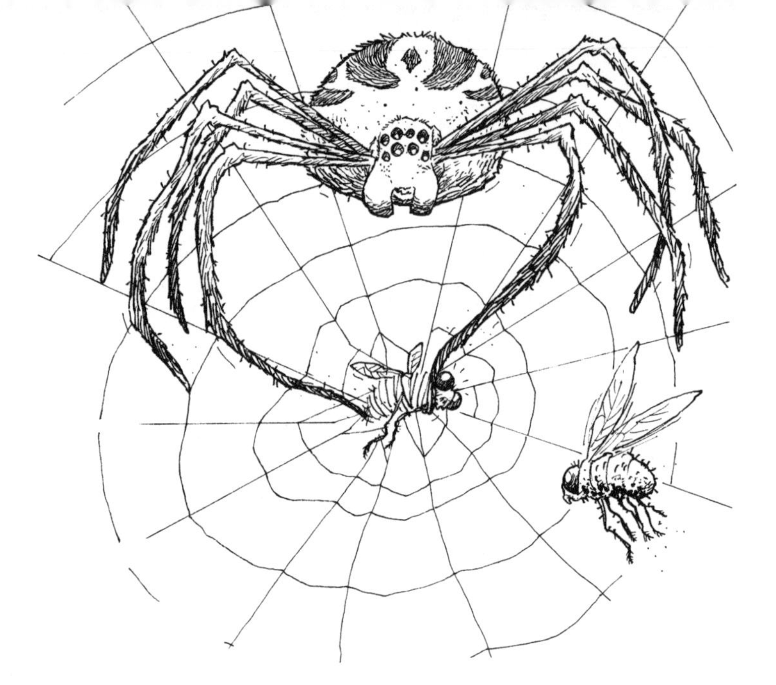

"Fly away!" called up Danny, in a rather muffled way. Several bands of silk were across his face. Josh did, whizzing up out of reach. Then the spider scuttled back down to her main course.

"It's all right, Danny," yelled down Josh, hovering above. "She won't kill you right away . . . she'll just . . . um . . . bite you . . . a bit . . ."

"A bit?" squawked Danny.

"Yeah . . . and paralyze you with her venom . . . and . . ."

"And?" mumbled Danny, through a mouthful of silk. "And what?"

"Make you runny before eating you."

"Well—thanks for that!" called back Danny. "Knowing exactly what to expect makes me feel so much better!"

"Don't worry—I'll rescue you!" called back Josh.

"Will you?" asked Danny. The lady spider lowered her brown and grey speckly face toward him. She slid a pair of fat fangs out of her mouthparts.

"No," admitted Josh.

Danny shut his eyes.

"But they will!" Josh yelled.

There was a crunching noise.

Danny opened his eyes just in time to see the spider's last leg disappearing into the furry face of . . .

"SCRATCH!" he yelled, joyfully. "SNIFF!" he added, just as joyfully. Another furry face appeared. Two giant brown rats were now peering at him with great concern. The last time he and Josh had met Scratch and Sniff, the rats had saved their lives. It looked as if it was becoming a habit!

"Careful now," said Scratch. "It's pretty delicate work, picking silk off a fly without picking the legs off with it. Normally we just eat flies still wrapped."

Danny hiccuped in fright. "Oh, don't be silly—I'm teasing you," laughed Scratch. "We don't eat flies. We and flies have a bond! Humans hate 'em as much as us! And all rats and flies do is tidy things up, you know. Clear up the gooey stuff that you don't want lying around. Nah. We get along all right, rats and flies. Want me to get a swarm together and have them attack that Petty Potts for you? Ow—this stuff is sticky!"

"Oh, move over! Let me!" said his wife. Sniff leaned over. She carefully began to unwind the silk with her delicate, long-nailed fingers.

Josh landed next to them. "You gobbled that spider in one munch!" he marveled. "I thought you two said you never ate spiders . . . the last time we met."

"Well, dear," said Sniff, still carefully unraveling Danny. "We were being polite. You were both spiders yourselves at the time."

"Don't really like 'em much," said Scratch. He picked a bit of thorax out of his teeth with a cough. "But can't have one of 'em eating an old friend, can we?"

"What are you both doing here?" asked Josh.

"Oh, just doing our rounds, love," said Sniff. "Always worth popping in when she's making cakes. We heard a bit of a to-do in here. We recognized your voices!"

"Thank you so much!" sighed Josh. "I thought Danny was done for this time."

"Well, he will be, if you hang around here much longer," said Scratch. He cast his beady eyes around the dark cave behind the sofa. "Plenty more spiders where that one came from. How come you let that mad scientist catch you and spray you again?"

"We didn't—I mean—we decided to spray ourselves, this time," said Danny. He got back up on his six feet and carefully flexed his wings.

"You must be stark-staring bonkers," said Sniff. She shook her head with a quiver of whiskers. "You nearly got eaten last time. And here you are nearly getting eaten again! Didn't you learn your lesson?"

Danny and Josh quickly explained their mission.

"So," said Scratch, "let me get this straight. You let Petty Potts turn you into flies so you could rescue some bits of twig for your mom?"

"Well . . . sort of," said Josh. He had to admit that it now seemed like a fairly silly idea. "We wanted to find out if they cut off Mom's birds. Now we know Tarquin cut the birds off. And now we've found them here, Mom might still be able to wire the twigs back on again if we can get them back."

"What—those bits of twigs that they're picking up and pulling apart now?" checked Scratch.

"NO!" shouted Josh and Danny, together.

"You've got to stop them! Please!" begged Josh. "We're too tiny to make any difference! Can you both create a distraction?"

Scratch and Sniff looked at each other, shrugged, and then ran out across the carpet.

"Eeeeek, eeeeek," said Scratch in a rather bored voice. Mrs. Sharpe whirled around, looked down, and began to shriek with horror. "Eee-eek. Look at me. I might be carrying the plague . . . "

He and his wife disappeared into the hallway, calling back, "Come on! Eeeeeek! Chase us!"

"How many times must I tell you," they heard Sniff scold him, "not to keep bringing up the plague?"

With much squealing and hand flapping, Mrs. Sharpe and Tarquin ran out after them.

Josh and Danny grinned at each other. Then they flew up away from the dusty, dark cave behind the sofa. From high up on the ceiling, they could see the hedge birds still lying on the floor. Only one of them had lost a wing.

"Let's fly back and get Petty to debug us. Then bring Mom around here fast to confront them before they have time to destroy the evidence!" said Danny.

"OK," said Josh. "If we can ever get Mom to believe us."

Danny zoomed across the room and out into the hallway. But Josh suddenly felt rather peculiar and heavy. One moment he was in the air, about to fly after his twin brother—the next . . .

Josh found himself face down on the swirly red carpet. He had just changed back into a boy! He sprang up and opened his mouth to shout to Danny. Then he realized that he couldn't. He was in Mrs. Sharpe's living room! She and Tarquin were just outside in the hall squawking about Scratch and Sniff.

"Let's get the poker and the coal tongs from the fire. We can beat them out with those!" shrieked Mrs. Sharpe.

And the living room door was flung open.

Happy Snappy

Josh hurled himself back behind the sofa—a much tighter fit this time—just as they walked in.

"Ugh! How disgusting!" shuddered Mrs. Sharpe. "We shall have to call in an exterminator. But how can we? The neighbors will see. I will be so humiliated. Imagine—rats! Vermin in my home—my garden!"

Josh stared through a narrow gap between the sofa and the wall. He watched them crouch down by the hedge birds. There was a whimpering noise.

"Oh for heaven's sake!" snapped Mrs. Sharpe. "Stop crying, Tarquin!"

"But, Mother! One of them scratched me when I tried to kick it. I might have caught the Black Death," sniffed Tarquin.

"For a genius, you really are an oaf, Tarquin!" was his mother's tender reply.

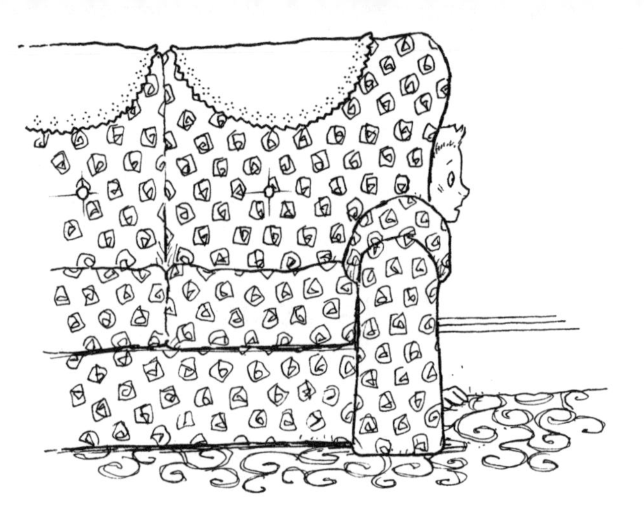

Jammed behind the sofa, Josh wondered what to do next. The evidence of cheating in the Best Garden Contest was right in front of him. But now he was trapped! The window was just above his head. But if he tried to escape through it, Mrs. Sharpe and Tarquin would see him. They could call the police and then hide the evidence of their own crime before the police arrived. Even with Danny backing him up, who was going to believe two eight-year-olds against Mrs. Sharpe and her son?

And where was Danny?

This was not going as planned. Not at all. Josh sighed. Then he felt something digging through his jeans pocket. His new camera! Josh grinned. He got the camera out and turned it on. He focused the zoom lens through the gap. Then he took a picture of Mrs. Sharpe and her son. Not a very flattering one . . .

"It's like a plague in here!" muttered Mrs. Sharpe. "First flies, then rats—whatever next? A swarm of locusts?" Just as she reached for Mom's favorite hedge bird her eyes widened and she paused.

"What was that clicking noise?"

"Locusts?" breathed Tarquin, looking scared.

"It came from behind the sofa!" she whispered. Mother and son turned to stare right at the spot where Josh was hidden. He could see them through the gap, but could they see him?

"Tarquin—go and look behind the sofa!" ordered Mrs. Sharpe.

"But—I don't want to!" wailed Tarquin. "It might be more rats . . ."

"If you want any dessert today, you'll do as you're told!" snapped his mother.

Tarquin crept toward the sofa. He curled his bony fingers across the top of it and pulled. Josh cringed. He was about to be found out, skulking behind the furniture in a neighbor's house, like a burglar.

"AAAARGH!" screamed Mrs. Sharpe. "RATS! RATS! THERE THEY GO AGAIN."

Josh laughed silently with relief. Scratch and Sniff had run into the room, done a loop around the carpet, and run off out again.

Mrs. Sharpe and Tarquin hurried out after them. Josh leapt to his feet, jumped over the sofa, and gathered Mom's hedge birds into the trash bag. He slung it over his shoulder and then climbed through the front room window. He landed on the immaculate front lawn. With Mrs. Sharpe's screams and Tarquin's shrieks echoing from the house, he ran for the gate and made straight for home.

As he reached the corner of the road, he ran right into Danny.

"There you are!" cried his brother. "We thought you'd been swatted!"

Petty could be seen hurrying along the road

behind Danny. "Oh, thank goodness!" she puffed. "You've not been eaten! Now—you naughty boys. Don't ever do such a thing ever again!"

Josh and Danny turned and gave her a very hard stare.

"Oh, all right," she muttered, adjusting her spectacles. "I just like to pretend to be a normal grown-up sometimes . . ."

Picture Perfect

The camera memory stick slid into Petty's computer. It clicked and whirred.

"It's very powerful but a bit slow," said Petty, in the green light of the laboratory.

"Um . . . one thing I've been wondering about . . . " ventured Danny.

"Yes, Danny?" said Petty. She pushed her glasses up her nose and jabbed at the keyboard.

"Why aren't I stark naked?"

Petty blinked in surprise. "Because it's a little chilly today?"

"No—I mean why aren't there a couple of piles of clothes in the plastic tent thingy where we got S.W.I.T.C.H.ed?" went on Danny. "When we turned into flies we should have flown right out of our pants, shouldn't we? And then, when we came back to being human, we should've been stark naked!"

Petty laughed. "A good point, Danny. It's to do with how S.W.I.T.C.H. works. It actually changes all your cells' energy patterns. And everything that's connected to them at the point when you are sprayed gets changed too."

"Energy patterns?" repeated Josh.

"Yes. All you need to know is that everything immediately connected to you changes with you. OK?"

Josh and Danny nodded, slowly.

"And a jolly good thing too," added Petty. "A pair of identical streaking eight-year-olds is the last thing we need when we're working together on a top secret project."

"Are we . . . ?" said Danny, looking at Josh.

"Working on a top secret project? With her?" Josh shrugged. He hadn't decided yet. No matter how exciting it was to think of being a dragon one day, it was just so dangerous. Only an hour ago, Danny had nearly been a spider's lunch!

There was a ping.

"Ah!" said Petty. "Here are your photos, Josh."

A series of photos opened up across her large screen. Josh's finger. Josh's eye. Danny, his head sideways, laughing hard at Josh for trying to take a photo with his new camera backward and sideways. Then pictures of Mom in the garden, a close-up of the rockery, Danny pretending to be a giant fly, Danny sitting up behind Jenny's shoulder, Jenny hitting him with her rolled-up magazine . . .

And then, three really clear shots of . . .

. . . a swirly red carpet.

"What?" squawked Josh. "Oh no! Where's Mrs. Sharpe and Tarquin? Now we've got no evidence!"

"You must have messed up the angle," muttered Danny. "What a waste of time!"

"Nonsense," said Petty Potts, leaning in close to peer at the photos. "You got the hedge birds back for your mom, didn't you?"

"Yes, but I wanted the police to go around and arrest Mrs. Sharpe and Tarquin!" huffed Josh.

Petty had maximized one photo on her computer so it filled the whole screen and was now peering so closely at it that her nose was against the monitor. "Who cares about them?" she said, with growing excitement in her voice. "Josh! Where is this?" She jabbed her finger at the picture of Mom's rock garden. Josh noticed, for the first time, that something bright was shining under one of the rocks. Probably a bit of a broken bottle.

"I took that in the front garden," said Josh. "Why?"

"Take me there! Right away!" demanded Petty, springing to her feet. Josh and Danny shrugged at each other and led the way. Two minutes

later, Petty Potts was on her hands and knees, scrabbling through the rockery. It was a good thing Mom had gone inside after wiring the hedge birds back on. She would have been horrified. But after just a few seconds, Petty leapt to her feet. She held up something covered in dirt. "YESS!" she cried. "Look! Josh! Danny! I can't believe it!"

They stared closely at the thing in her hand. Some of the loose dirt fell away from it. It was a glass cube.

"Wow—it's—it's one of those S.W.I.T.C.H. cube thingies!" breathed Danny.

Now he could see a holographic image inside the glass. It looked a bit like an alligator.

Petty Potts held the cube to her cheek. "Another REPTOSWITCH cube! I knew they couldn't be far away! I knew it. Now . . . if only I could remember where I'd hidden the rest."

"Are you sure you hid them?" said Josh.

"Yes—my memory is burnt out in places, as you know. But I remember hiding the cubes where I could find them later in an emergency. There are another four of these—the REPTOSWITCH ones—hidden somewhere near the lab," explained Petty.

"Except you forgot where," pointed out Danny.

"Yes! Exactly! So far, I've only managed to find the cubes with the BUGSWITCH code. All the others have been lost for years! And that's why I need your help. Will you look for REPTOSWITCH cubes for me?" asked Petty, smiling at them hopefully. (She looked less like a spider in a web this time.)

"Look," said Josh. "We will help you. We will look for your cubes. But we won't change into any more bugs. OK?"

"Absolutely fine!" said Petty. "I would never dream of asking you to."

She put the glass cube in her pocket. She put her rather muddy fingers on each of their heads.

"Josh—Danny. Welcome to the S.W.I.T.C.H. Project!"

Flying Finish

"Well, this is lovely, I must say!" The Best Garden judge smiled approvingly at the garden. "I particularly like these!" he added, patting the hedge birds. "They must have taken years to grow and cut into such delightful shapes." Around the judge, the crowd murmured, impressed.

"Oh yes—years," agreed Mom, smiling back, nervously. "But I have to admit to you that yesterday somebody came along and chopped them off. I had to wire them back on."

The crowd gasped and the judge's eyebrows rose up. "They won't last, of course," went on Mom. "In a week the leaves will have died, but for now they look fine. I hope it won't mean I'm disqualified, but I'd rather not pretend." She was still amazed that the hedge birds had been returned. Josh and Danny had run into the house to tell her that the hedge birds were lying on the garden path yesterday afternoon.

"Well—I think it's very good of you to be so honest," said the judge. "I certainly won't disqualify you over someone else's nasty trick."

The crowd walked on, and Mom, Josh, and Danny walked on too. They watched as the judge inspected other gardens in the competition.

Petty Potts suddenly arrived behind Josh and Danny. They smiled at her, glumly. How they wished Josh's photo of Mrs. Sharpe and Tarquin with the hedge birds had come out. They'd spent all morning grumbling about it, sitting by the shed in the backyard. Even when Scratch and Sniff had shown up (they lived under the shed) and sat on their shoulders for a while, they felt sad. The rats shook their furry little heads when Josh told them what had happened. "I can't stand to think of that stuck-up Mrs. Sharpe winning the prize!" said Danny. Scratch and Sniff squeaked at each other. Then they vanished back under the shed just as Mom came down the garden to tell Josh and

Danny the judging was starting.

Now the crowd gathered at Mrs. Sharpe's garden while the judge walked around it.

"You know, I don't think you really wanted to get the police involved, anyway," Petty muttered. "After all, they would have wondered how you came to be inside the Sharpes' house. It's for the best."

Mrs. Sharpe's garden was very neat with carefully arranged plants and flowers, a perfect lawn, and a water feature with a little fountain. Mrs. Sharpe stood at her gate, wearing a wide-brimmed hat, waving white-gloved hands, and nodding at everyone, as if she were the queen.

"Very good, as usual, Mrs. Sharpe," beamed the judge, after looking around for a few minutes. "Always one of our star gardens. Quite immaculate."

"Well, you know I cannot bear untidiness or unpleasantness in a garden," simpered Mrs. Sharpe. "For me, there has to be perfect order. Nothing less." Tarquin stood behind her. He wore a neat navy-blue suit and a smug smile.

"Well," said the judge. "As this is our last garden, I think I can now announce the winner."

An expectant hush fell upon the crowd, broken only by the buzzing of a few flies. Then a few more flies. And a bit more buzzing.

The judge fanned his face. "Gosh! Your garden is a haven for insect life, Mrs. Sharpe."

"Well—butterflies and bees, of course," trilled Mrs. Sharpe. She swiped something off her chin.

"No—bluebottles and cluster flies," said Josh.

He grinned. There were a lot of flies. Really quite a swarm in fact. Someone gave a little scream. There were now clouds of flies all over Mrs. Sharpe's garden. They settled on her neat borders and danced around her little fountain.

"They're attracted to garbage, old meat, dog poo. That kind of stuff," Josh cheerily informed the crowd.

"I don't have garbage or old meat or dog poo in my garden!" exclaimed Mrs. Sharpe.

"Well, you must have. You've certainly got vermin!" pointed out Petty. And there—running around the fountain—were Scratch and Sniff.

They raced up and down the lawn, squeaking, and swirling cyclones of flies followed them.

As the crowd turned panicky, Josh and Danny were doubled up laughing. Scratch and Sniff had obviously decided to help out, after hearing Josh and Danny's bad news earlier.

"Of course!" Josh giggled, wildly, to Danny and Petty. "Scratch told us he could get flies to swarm for him. Now he's proved it!"

Everyone was now edging quickly away from Mrs. Sharpe's garden.

"Wait! Wait!" she squealed after them, swatting flies off her clothes in crazy swoops. "I've made tea! I've made cakes! Scones and jam . . . to celebrate my victory . . ."

"Nothing to celebrate this year, Mrs. Sharpe," called back the judge, scribbling on his clipboard as he ran down the road. "You came in ninth! Better get an exterminator in for those rats!"

"But I don't have rats! I don't!" sobbed Mrs. Sharpe, twitching and dancing while Tarquin slapped his face repeatedly.

Josh stayed long enough to take a photograph. He got the angle right this time.

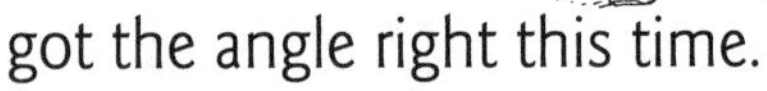

"Good old Scratch and Sniff!" cheered Danny as their furry friends disappeared behind Mrs. Sharpe's greenhouse.

Back at the Phillips's yard, Mom was being cheered by the crowd. She'd won! Even Jenny came outside to join in the celebration.

"Ugh! Flies! How disgusting!" she squealed, when she heard about the drama. "I bet Danny freaked out."

"Nope," said Danny. "Flies are brilliant. I will never squash a fly again. Flies are my friends." He wandered off as Petty sidled up to Josh.

"So—are you both quite all right?" she checked, peering at him closely. "No aftereffects?"

"Not me," said Josh. He pointed at Danny. "Not so sure about him though . . ."

Danny's nose twitched as he stared longingly at the trash can. Danny began to drool.

"Danneeeeee!" called Josh.

"I—can't—help—it . . ." wailed Danny, running his hands over the lid.

"SPIDER!" shouted Josh. Danny hurtled off the trash can and ran into the house. He nearly collided with Jenny as she walked back toward the house.

"Oh why must you always bug me?" yelled Jenny. "And what are you doing over there, Josh?"

"Um . . . nothing," said Josh, sniffing at the trash can lid. He ran after Danny before he could give in to the urge to lick the gooey bits. "Gotta fly!"

Top Secret!

For Petty Potts's Eyes Only!!

DIARY ENTRY *575.3

SUBJECT: Josh and Danny Phillips's Recruitment

Good work! Have convinced Josh and Danny to join me in the S.W.I.T.C.H. Project. They don't seem to have suffered any bad side effects from their latest S.W.I.T.C.H. Apart from wanting to eat out of trash cans.

Josh is the smarter one and really knows his wildlife. He should be quite a help in making notes. Danny is bright too, though. He's very brave, considering he is actually quite scared of bugs and insects.

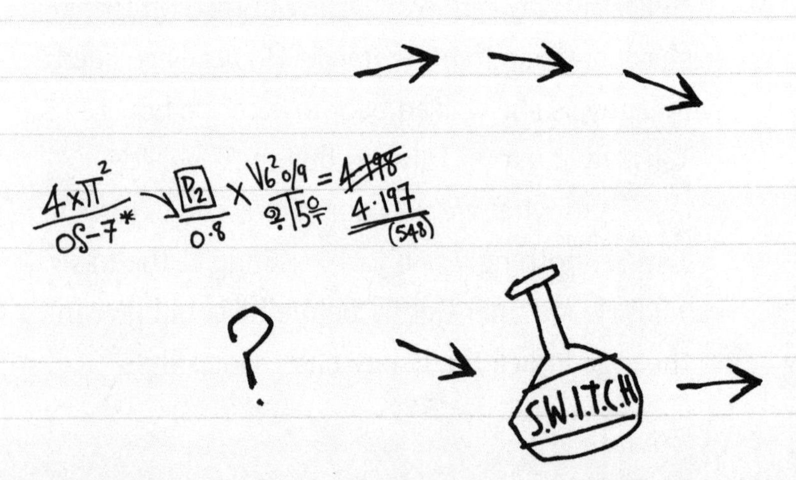

Of course, most importantly, they are four extra eyes in the search for the missing REPTOSWITCH cubes. We found one today! Now I have two out of six. If Josh and Danny can help me find the other four, I will be able to advance the project to the reptilian level!

I haven't told them the whole story yet.

They know about Victor Crouch—the rotten thief. But they don't know that I think he may be watching me. That's the main reason I can't search too hard for the REPTOSWITCH cubes myself, of course. If Victor or one of his spies sees me looking, they will realize that there are more cubes and start looking too. But Josh and Danny can search the whole street! Because none of Victor's spies will ever suspect two eight-year-old boys, will they?

REPTOSWITCH! Here we come!

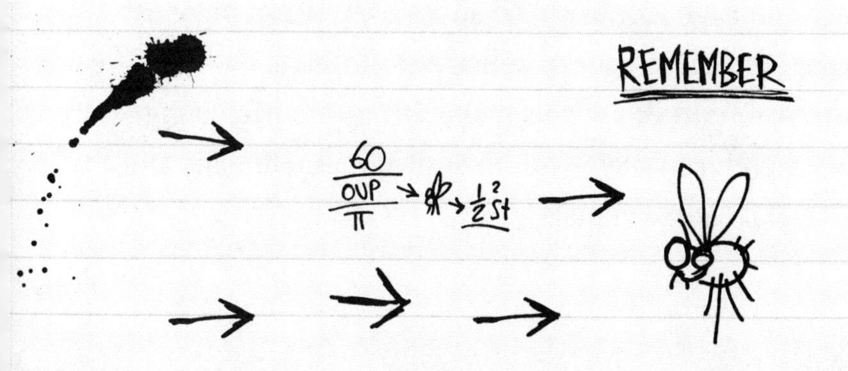

Glossary

antennae: long, thin feelers, protruding from an insect's forehead. Flies use their antennae to smell and feel their surroundings.

bluebottle: a type of fly with a metallic blue and green thorax. Bluebottles are covered in black bristly hairs. They make a noisy buzzing sound when they fly. They are about half an inch long.

cellular: something made from a group of living cells

hexagonal: a shape that has six sides

hijack: to take control of something by force

hologram: a picture made up of laser beams that appear three-dimensional (3-D)

insect: animals with six legs and three body parts—the head, the thorax, and the abdomen

locusts: insects that breed very quickly and fly in large groups called swarms. A swarm of locusts can cause a lot of damage to crops.

mammal: animals that give birth to live young and feed them with their own milk. Humans and rats are mammals.

palps: feelers that spiders use to search for food
plague: sometimes known as the Black Death, the plague was a serious illness. Fleas living on rats carried the disease and spread it to humans.
proboscis: a long sucking organ or mouthpart. Flies use their proboscis to suck up food.
reptiles: cold-blooded animals. Lizards and snakes are reptiles.
thorax: the section of an insect's body between the head and abdomen
topiary: pruning (or trimming) bushes and hedges into attractive shapes
vermin: animals or insects that can damage crops or carry disease. Rats are often described as vermin.

Recommended Reading

BOOKS

Want to brush up on your bug knowledge? Here's a list of books dedicated to creepy-crawlies.

Glaser, Linda. *Not a Buzz to Be Found.* Minneapolis: Millbrook Press, 2012.

Heos, Bridget. *What to Expect When You're Expecting Larvae: A Guide for Insect Parents (and Curious Kids).* Minneapolis: Millbrook Press, 2011.

Markle, Sandra. Insect World series. Minneapolis: Lerner Publications, 2008.

WEBSITES

Find out more about nature and wildlife using the websites below.

BioKids

http://www.biokids.umich.edu/critters/

The University of Michigan's Critter Catalog has a ton of pictures of different kinds of bugs and information on where they live, how they behave, and their predators.

National Geographic Kids

http://video.nationalgeographic.com/video/kids/animals-pets-kids/bugs-kids
Go to this fun website to watch clips from National Geographic about all sorts of creepy-crawlies.

U.S. Fish & Wildlife Service

http://www.fws.gov/letsgooutside/kids.html
This website has lots of activities for when you're outside playing and looking for wildlife.

CHECK OUT ALL OF THE

#1 Spider Stampede

Eight-year-olds Josh and Danny discover that their neighbor Miss Potts has a secret formula that can change people into bugs. Soon enough, they find themselves with six extra legs. Can the boys survive in the world as spiders long enough to make it home in time for dinner?

#2 Fly Frenzy

Danny and Josh are avoiding their neighbor because she "accidentally" turned them into bugs. But when their mom's garden is ruined the day before a big competition, the twins turn into bluebottle houseflies to discover the culprits. Will they find who's responsible before it's too late?

#3 Grasshopper Glitch

Danny and Josh are having a normal day at school . . . until they turn into grasshoppers in the middle of class! Can they avoid being eaten during their whirlwind search to find the antidote? And will they be able to change back before getting a week of detention?

TITLES!

#4 Ant Attack

Danny and Josh are being forced to play with Tarquin, the most annoying boy in the neighborhood. But things get dangerous when the twins accidentally turn into ants and discover that Tarquin kills bugs for fun. . . . Can they find a safe place to hide until they turn human again?

#5 Crane Fly Crash

When Petty Potts leaves town, she puts Danny and Josh in charge of some of her S.W.I.T.C.H. spray. Unfortunately, their sister, Jenny, mistakes it for hair spray and ends up as a crane fly. Now it's up to the twins to keep Jenny from being eaten alive.

#6 Beetle Blast

Danny is forced to go with his brother, Josh, to his nature group, but neither of them thought they would turn into the nature they were studying! Both brothers become beetles just in time to learn about pond dipping . . . from the bug's perspective. Can they avoid getting caught by the other kids?

About the Author

Ali Sparkes grew up in the woods of Hampshire, England. Actually, strictly speaking, she grew up in a house in Hampshire. The woods were great but lacked basic facilities like sofas and a well-stocked fridge. Nevertheless, the woods were where she and her friends spent much of their time, and so Ali grew up with a deep and abiding love of wildlife. If you ever see Ali with a large garden spider on her shoulder, she will most likely be screeching, "AAAARRRGHGETITOFFME!"

Ali lives in Southampton with her husband and sons. She would never kill a creepy-crawly of any kind. They are more scared of her than she is of them. (Creepy-crawlies, not her husband and sons.)

About the Illustrator

Ross Collins's more than eighty picture books and books for young readers have appeared in print around the world. He lives in Scotland and, in his spare time, enjoys leaning backward precariously in his chair.